The Chanukkah Tree

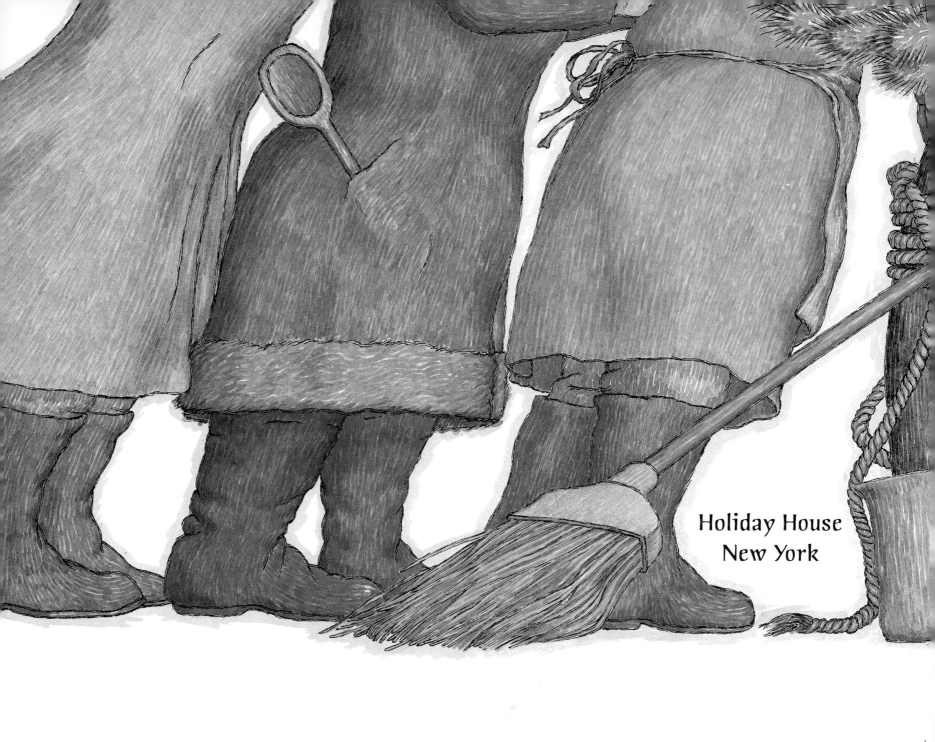

Holiday House
New York

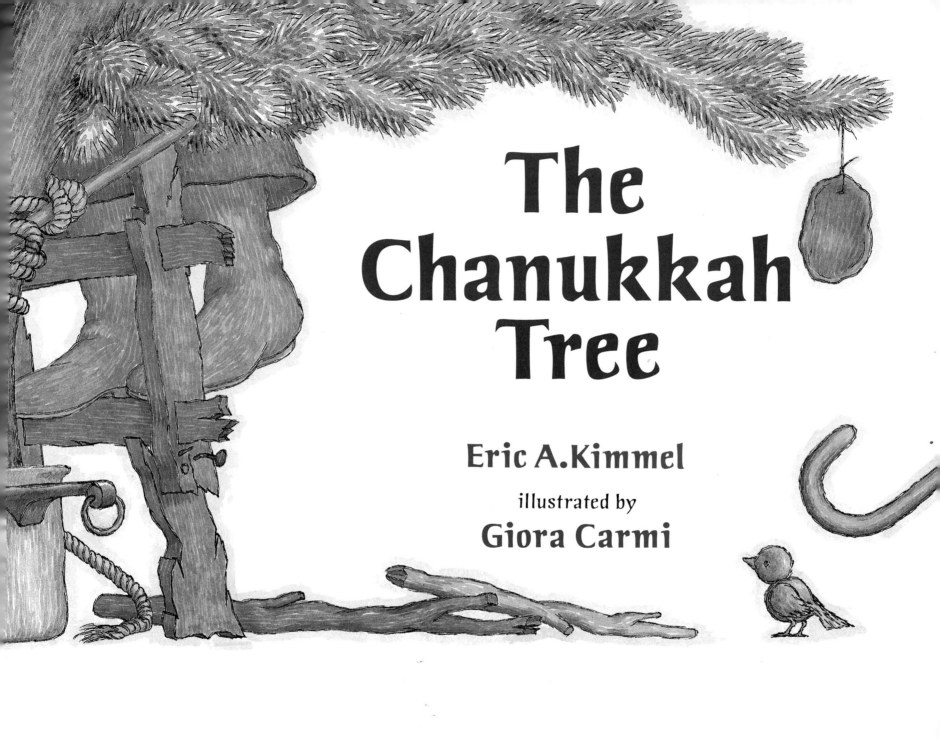

The
Chanukkah
Tree

Eric A. Kimmel

illustrated by
Giora Carmi

This story first appeared in
Cricket, the Magazine for Children.

Text copyright © 1987 by Eric A. Kimmel
Illustrations copyright © 1988 by Giora Carmi
All rights reserved
Printed in the United States of America
First Edition

Library of Congress Cataloging-in-Publication Data

Kimmel, Eric A.
The Chanukkah tree.

Summary: The foolish people of Chelm are tricked
by a peddler into buying and decorating a "Chanukkah
tree" on Christmas Eve, but after becoming disillusioned
they rediscover its worth and beauty.
[1. Hanukkah—Fiction.   2. Jews—Fiction]
I. Carmi, Giora, ill.   II. Title.
PZ7.K5648Ch   1988   [E]   88-4510
ISBN 0-8234-0705-5

Favel the town clerk

Mendel the butcher

Rivi, the baker's wife

To Dad

the rabbi

Yudel
the mayor

Haskel
the tailor

Isaac
the blacksmith

One Christmas Eve, a peddler drove his wagon down the road. In the back was a beautiful Christmas tree which he had tried hard to sell all day. By now it was late in the evening and every home already had its tree. The peddler was so disappointed. He hated to throw such a beautiful tree away, but unless he could sell it, what else could he do? He decided to continue down the road to the town of Chelm. The people of Chelm were Jewish, he knew, and did not celebrate Christmas. But he also knew something else. The people of Chelm were not very clever.

"A tree for sale! A beautiful tree for sale! Who will buy this beautiful tree?" the peddler cried as he drove his wagon into Chelm's main square.

The people of Chelm laughed. "A tree? Everyone in this town is Jewish. We celebrate Chanukkah, not Christmas. What do we want with a Christmas tree?"

"Who said anything about a Christmas tree?" the peddler replied. "Can't I see the menorahs in your windows? I know you're Jewish. That's why I brought you this Chanukkah tree."

A Chanukkah tree? The people of Chelm had never heard of such a thing. They stared at each other, then at the peddler.

"That's right," the peddler continued. "A Chanukkah tree. From America. Over there Chanukkah trees are the latest thing. Every Jewish home has one."

"Really?" This news surprised the people of Chelm. They had never heard of a Chanukkah tree, but they knew that anything from America must be modern and up-to-date. "What do you do with a Chanukkah tree?" they asked.

"What do you do with a Chanukkah tree?" the peddler exclaimed, as if surprised to find a town that had never heard of one. "First, you wind it all around with strings of popcorn and berries. Then you hang ornaments from its branches. Then you decorate it with colored lights. Finally, at the very top, you put a big star."

"That sounds like a Christmas tree," one little boy said.

"It is," said the peddler. "Only better!"

By the time the peddler finished his speech, the people of Chelm were sold. Chelm had to have a Chanukkah tree. They bought it from the peddler, took it off the wagon, and set it up in the middle of the town square. The peddler drove off with their money in his pocket, chuckling to himself. "A Chanukkah tree! Only in Chelm!"

The people of Chelm looked at their tree. "What do we do with it?" Haskel the tailor asked.

"Remember, the peddler said to wind it all around with strings of popcorn and berries," Mendel the butcher answered.

"But we don't have any popcorn, and we already used the berries to make jam for our potato latkes," Isaac the blacksmith pointed out.

"Wait!" said Yudel the mayor. "I know what to do. We may not have popcorn and berries, but we do have lots of potato latkes. What else for a Chanukkah tree but latkes!"

Everybody ran home and got potato latkes. They tied the latkes to the Chanukkah tree's branches.

"That looks better," Yudel said. "But something's still missing."

"I know what it is," said Favel, the town clerk. "Ornaments. The peddler said that in America they decorate the Chanukkah tree with ornaments."

"What kind of ornaments?" the people asked.

"Who knows?" said Favel. "But I can't think of better ornaments for a Chanukkah tree than dreidels. We have plenty of dreidels. Let's decorate the Chanukkah tree with dreidels!"

The people of Chelm thought that was a wonderful idea. They ran home and got dreidels: wooden dreidels, tin dreidels, clay dreidels. They tied the dreidels to the branches of the Chanukkah tree.

"This is turning into a beautiful tree!" Haskel the tailor said. "What else did the peddler say we needed?"

"He mentioned something about colored lights," said Isaac the blacksmith.

"Lights!" said Yudel the mayor. "That's easy. We all have plenty of Chanukkah candles. Let's go home and get them."

All the people ran home to get candles. They set them in the branches of the Chanukkah tree. Soon the whole tree was lit from top to bottom.

"Is this a tree!" Rivi, the baker's wife, sighed. "I can't imagine a better Chanukkah tree than this. Not even in America."

"But what about the star?" Abraham the schoolteacher asked.

"Star? What star?"

"Don't you remember? The peddler said to put a big star on the top of the tree."

"Ah, yes," the people of Chelm remembered. But where could they get a star?

"I know," said the rabbi, fingering his long white beard. "The biggest star in town is right over there. Look!" He pointed to the heavy oak door of the synagogue and to the six-pointed Jewish star that was carved on it.

"A star!" the people cried. They quickly took the synagogue door from its hinges, star and all, and tied it to the top of the Chanukkah tree.

Now the decorations were finished. The people of Chelm filled the town square as they stood and admired the Chanukkah tree.

"Imagine! A Chanukkah tree! In Chelm!"

"Where do they think of such things?"

"Only in America!"

"Ha! America has nothing on us!"

Although it was late, the people of Chelm were so proud of their Chanukkah tree they didn't want to go to bed. They stood in the town square waiting for a traveler to come by so they could show off their tree.

Just before midnight a man driving an automobile came bumping down the road. Even though it was just beginning to snow, the people of Chelm ran out to greet him. "Happy Chanukkah! Happy Chanukkah!" they cried.

The man stopped the automobile, rolled down the window, and stared. Standing before his eyes was the oddest tree he had ever seen. Potato latkes and dreidels hung from its branches. Dozens of tiny candles gleamed among its needles. Tied to its top was an enormous door.

"What is it?" the man asked.

"Can't you guess? It's a Chanukkah tree! It's our Chanukkah tree!" the people of Chelm said with pride.

"Chanukkah tree? I never heard of such a thing," said the man.

"It's a new custom," Yudel the mayor explained. "It comes from America. All the Jewish people there have Chanukkah trees."

"No they don't!" the man cried. "I come from America. I've never heard of a Chanukkah tree."

"You haven't?" Yudel asked. "Then how do the people there celebrate Chanukkah?"

The man laughed. "Why, the same way Jewish people everywhere celebrate Chanukkah! With potato latkes, dreidels, menorahs. But not with trees. Jewish people don't have trees. There's no such thing as a Chanukkah tree." The man shook his head, started his automobile, and drove off.

The people of Chelm stood in the town square. They were so shocked they couldn't think of a single word to say. They didn't know what to do. At last the rabbi spoke. "Did you hear what that man said? He said he comes from America. He said he's never heard of a Chanukkah tree."

"He said there's no such thing as a Chanukkah tree," said Rivi, the baker's wife. She still didn't believe her ears.

Favel, the town clerk, scratched his head. "But we certainly have a tree. Here it stands in the middle of our town. If it's not a Chanukkah tree, what kind of tree is it?"

"I'll tell you what kind of tree it is," Isaac the blacksmith said bitterly. "It's a fool tree, and we're the fools! That peddler was a swindler. He's probably still laughing at us."

The people of Chelm knew Isaac was right. They were so upset about being fooled that they couldn't bear to look at the tree. Disgusted, they turned their backs on it, went home, and went to bed.

Just before dawn, they woke to the sound of birds singing. The people of Chelm got out of bed, put on their clothes, and ran to their windows to see what was happening. They had never heard so many birds singing at once; not at this time of year, in the dead of winter.

A heavy snow had fallen during the night. It covered everything. But there in the center of town stood the Chanukkah tree with dozens and dozens of birds perched in its branches. Dozens more pecked at the ground around its base. The people of Chelm ran outside for a better look. Where had all these birds come from?

"It was the tree!" Favel, the town clerk, realized. "The synagogue door made a roof to shelter them from the snow. The candles kept them warm, and the potato latkes fed them."

The birds flew around the square, chirping and singing.

"Listen to them!" cried Rivi, the baker's wife. "It sounds as if the birds are singing, 'Happy Chanukkah, people of Chelm! Happy Chanukkah!'"

"Happy Chanukkah! Happy Chanukkah, birds!" the people of Chelm cried.

"Imagine," the rabbi said, stroking his long beard as he watched the birds fly about the square. "A Chanukkah tree in Chelm. It must be the only one of its kind. Nobody else has a Chanukkah tree. Not even in America."

The people of Chelm were so proud of their Chanukkah tree that they decided to make one every year as a special present for their friends, the birds.

The tree stands in the town square with the big synagogue door and its six-pointed star tied to the top. Its branches are hung with potato latkes and dreidels and lit with Chanukkah candles from top to bottom. Those who have seen it say there is nothing like it anywhere in the world. Not even in America.

A Chanukkah tree?

Only in Chelm.